Bun's New Hats
A lesson on self-esteem

by Suzanne I. Barchers
illustrated by Mattia Cerato

RED
CHAIR
•PRESS•

Please visit our website at **www.redchairpress.com**.
Find a free catalog of all our high-quality products for young readers.

Bun's New Hats
Library of Congress Control Number: 2012931798
ISBN: 978-1-937529-15-4 (pbk)
ISBN: 978-1-937529-23-9 (hc)

Lexile is a registered trademark of MetaMetrics, Inc. Used with permission.
Leveling provided by Linda Cornwell of Literacy Connections Consulting.

This edition first published in 2012 by
Red Chair Press, LLC   PO Box 333   South Egremont, MA 01258-0333

Printed in China
1   2   3   4   5   16   15   14   13   12

Bun

Pip

Sox

Tab

Ted

Bun's New Hats

Bun loves her silly hats! Then she hears her friends make fun of how they look. When the friends learn that Bun's feelings are hurt, they must decide how to make it up to her.

Sox stops at Tab's house. "Can we go for a run?"
Tab says with a yawn, "Can't we nap in the sun?"

"Come on, Tab," says Sox. "It's a beautiful day."
"Alright," says Tab. "Let's be on our way."

Bun hops in their pathway. They stop in surprise.
When they see her hat, they can't believe their eyes!

"Do you like my new hat?" Bun proudly cries.
"Uh...it's very pretty," Sox quickly lies.

The two friends run off. Bun stays behind.
Tab talks as they run, "Sox, you were too kind.

That hat's really silly. It's also too big.
It looks like something you'd put on a pig!"

Bun heard every word. Her eyes fill with tears.
She wishes she didn't have such great big ears.

"I'll make something better!" Bun says with a shout.
"I just need an idea that will make me stand out."

The very next day, Bun sees Pip and Ted.
They stop. They stare. "What's that on your head?"

12

"It's uh...different," Pip says, hiding her frown.
"I knew you would like it," Bun says. "It's a crown!"

"Where did you get it?" Ted says with a giggle.
"I made it!" Bun says, as her crown starts to wiggle.

"Come run with us," Ted says. "It'll be fun."
Bun sighs, "With this crown, I can't really run."

"That crown looks so dumb," Ted says to Pip.
"Each time she moves, the crown starts to slip."

Bun hops home slowly, thinking things through.
By the time she gets home, she knows what to do.

The very next day, Bun hops down the path.
When her pals see Bun, they try not to laugh.

"What have you done?" Tab says with a snort.
"You've covered your ears. They look very short."

"I heard what you said about my hat and my crown. Tab said I looked silly. That made me feel down.

Ted said it looked dumb when we met yesterday.
With earmuffs, I won't always hear what you say."

"Oh, Bun! We're so sorry! Please do not cry.
I thought it was better to tell a little white lie.

You don't need a crown or a hat to look great.
Your ears are the best. They are really first-rate!"

The very next day, Bun hops down the path.
When she sees her friends, she tries not to laugh.

"You're the best!" Bun says to Pip, Sox, Tab, and Ted.
A silly, fun hat sits on every friend's head!

Big Questions:

How do you think Bun feels when she wears her silly hats? Do you have favorite things to wear?

Why did Bun get sad? What did the friends do to make Bun feel good again?

Big Words:

first-rate: of the best; excellent

proudly: done with happiness or pleasure

sighs: speaks with sadness or when tired

When Sox tells Bun her hat is pretty, the story says he told a "little white lie." Did telling a lie protect Bun's feelings? Is it ever okay to tell a lie?

Were the friends making fun of Bun when they showed up wearing silly hats too? Why do you think they did that?

Ask a parent or adult to help you find an old hat or cap that isn't worn much now. Think about what you like and find items to decorate or glue to the hat. It might be feathers, sports stickers and tickets, pictures from a magazine, or pine cones and leaves. Now you have your own silly hat!

About the Author

Suzanne I. Barchers, Ed.D., began a career in writing and publishing after fifteen years as a teacher. She has written over 100 children's books, two college textbooks, and more than 20 reader's theater and teacher resource books. She previously held editorial roles at Weekly Reader and LeapFrog and is on the PBS Kids Media Advisory Board for the next generation of children's programming. Suzanne also plays the flute professionally—and for fun—from her home in Stanford, CA.

About the Illustrator

Mattia Cerato was born in Cuneo, a small town in northern Italy where he still lives and works. As soon as he could hold a pencil he loved sketching things he saw around him. When he is not drawing, Mattia loves traveling around the world, reading good books, and playing and listening to cool music.

 For a free activity page for this story, go to www.redchairpress.com and look for Free Activities.

28